FOR NORMAN

Copyright © 1998 by Niki Daly
By arrangement with The Inkman, Cape Town, South Africa
All rights reserved
Hand-lettering by Andrew van der Merwe
First published in Great Britain by Frances Lincoln Limited, 1998
Printed in Hong Kong
First American edition, 1998

Library of Congress Cataloging-in-Publication Data
Daly, Niki.
Bravo, Zan Angelo! : a commedia dell'arte tale with story &
pictures / by Niki Daly. — 1st American ed.
        p. cm.
Summary: In Renaissance Venice, Angelo, longing to be as famous
a clown as his grandfather, decides to do something special with his
small part in his grandfather's commedia dell'arte production during
Carnival.
ISBN 0-374-30953-1
[1. Clowns—Fiction.   2. Grandfathers—Fiction.   3. Street
theater—Fiction.   4. Carnival—Italy—Venice—Fiction]   I. Title.
PZ7.D1715Br 1998
[E]—dc21   97-39436

Bravo, Zan Angelo!

A COMMEDIA DELL'ARTE TALE

with

STORY & PICTURES

by

Niki Daly

Farrar, Straus & Giroux · New York

Some mornings, Venice is brushed with golden sunlight.

If there's a mist, the silken lagoon turns pearly green. On such a morning, a long time ago, a boy called Angelo Polo walked along the water's edge toward the Piazza San Marco.

Bellissimo! The sights of San Marco's great square on the first day of Carnival could steal your breath away. The piazza was alive with laughter and music. There were puppet shows and conjurers. Lions roared in cages and monkeys danced up poles. The stages were filled with musicians, singers, and, best of all, clowns—*commedia dell'arte* clowns who juggled, tumbled, and buffooned, clowns who could make you weep with laughter.

Angelo wanted to be a clown like his grandfather Zan Polo. Zan Polo had once been the most famous clown in Venice. But, sadly, times had changed. Crowds no longer flocked to see his troupe perform, and Zan Polo had become a crusty old man who complained about this one, that one, and his old back, which had lost its spring.

So when he saw his grandson approaching, he barked, "Angelo, go home!" But Angelo, being a chip off the old block, went up to him and said, "I want to be a clown!"

"There is no place in my theater for a little boy," snapped Zan Polo.

"But," said Angelo, "I could be Arlecchino."

"Arlecchino must be tall and able to leap like a hare. You are short and look like a rabbit!" replied Zan Polo.

"Why can't I play the Captain?" asked Angelo. "I'd make a good Captain."
"Captain Cocodrillo must be built like a castle and have a voice like thunder,"
said Zan Polo. "You are skinny and twitter like a sparrow."

"What about Pantalone?" cried Angelo. "I want to be Pantalone!"
"Pantalone must be old, and you are a puppy," said Zan Polo.

"Then could I be the doctor who rides on the donkey?" asked Angelo.

"Dr. Balanzone must be able to recite the names and diseases of a hundred patients. You can barely count to ten," said Zan Polo. He was growing tired of this game.

But Angelo wouldn't stop. "Why can't I be Pulcinella?" he asked.

"Because *I* am Pulcinella!" shouted Zan Polo.

"Then who can I be?" cried Angelo.

Exasperated, Zan Polo bellowed,

"You can be the little red rooster who crows in the last act!"

There was, of course, no such part in the commedia dell'arte, and Angelo knew it.

"I don't want to play the little red rooster who crows in the last act," he said sadly.

Zan Polo softened a little. He said, "It's not what you play — it's how you play it that counts." Then, pulling down his black Pulcinella mask, he did a funny chicken walk and crowed.

"Can *I* crow on the stage?" asked Angelo.

"You can crow behind the backdrop," said Zan Polo.

"Lots and lots of times?" asked Angelo.

"Only once. Now, see that you are back here when the clock tower bell strikes three."

And that was that.

Angelo hurried off to Zanetti the mask maker. Inside his dimly lit workroom, painted masks glittered and hollow eyes stared out of dark corners. Yet nowhere could Angelo find what he was looking for.

Finally, he asked, "Signor Zanetti, do you have a little red rooster mask?"

The mask maker smiled. "I've never heard of such a mask," he replied, "but if you do some polishing for me, I'll see what I can do."

While Angelo polished a pile of leather masks, Zanetti cut, shaped, and trimmed bits of red and yellow leather.

The clock tower bell rang once. When Angelo looked up, Zanetti was holding out a beaked mask. It looked splendid!

"Grazie, Signore," said Angelo.

"Prego!" replied Zanetti.

Angelo skipped along canals and over bridges until he reached a little shop off the Campo Santo Stefano. Here, Signora Rocco sat among mountains of satin ribbons and patterned cloth, cutting and stitching Carnival costumes.

"Signora, do you have something for a little red rooster to wear?" asked Angelo.

"Don't bother me now, Angelo. There's a masked ball in the Palazzo Rezzonico tonight and I am up to my ears in sewing," she said. But when she saw Angelo's disappointed look, she cried, "Wait—I think I see a rooster's tail in the red coat you're wearing!" She bunched and tied up Angelo's coattails with a red rag until they stood out like the proudest plumes a rooster could wish for. Then she fastened a scrap of frill around Angelo's neck. "Now off with you, my little red rooster!" she said, smiling.

In the distance, the clock tower bell struck two. There was no time to waste! Angelo ran off to his Aunt Rosabella's house. Zia Rosabella kept a yard filled with fat hens and a terrifying rooster called Bardolino.

When his aunt saw Angelo coming into the yard, she roared with laughter. "Just wait till Bardolino sees you. Won't he be jealous!" she cried.

At the sight of a new rooster, Bardolino gave chase. "Cock-a-doodle-doo!"

Round and round they flew, until Angelo could outflap, outsquawk,
and even outcrow Bardolino.

Now Angelo was ready to show Zan Polo what he could do. Off he sped,
back to the Piazza San Marco, where the Carnival flowed like rich red
Bardolino wine.

Angelo squeezed through the river of people seeping down the narrow streets toward San Marco. With a push and a shove, he forced his way into the piazza just as the clock tower bell struck three.

Suddenly he collided with an elegantly dressed gentleman.

"Mi scusi!" gasped Angelo.

The stranger helped Angelo to his feet, dusted him off, and looked him up and down, smiling. He slipped off one of his red velvet gloves and placed it on Angelo's head. "A fine cockscomb for an elegant fowl!" he said.

Angelo bowed politely. Then he turned and darted toward the stage.

Angelo stood behind the backdrop, waiting his turn.

After a while, he decided to take a peek through a slit in the backdrop.

Laughter rippled through the audience when the little red rooster's head appeared.

Oh good! thought Angelo. They like me!

Encouraged by the laughter, Angelo pushed his way through the slit in the backdrop.

More laughs.

Then he broke into a little red rooster strut and swaggered right across the stage, swishing his tail and pumping his arms just like Bardolino.

"Bravo!" shouted the crowd.

At the front of the stage, Zan Polo, who was playing Pulcinella, beamed, thinking they were applauding him. Things *are* going well, he thought.

At that moment, Angelo let go a mighty "COCK-A-DOODLE-DOO!"
right behind his grandfather.

Zan Polo swung around, then froze at the sight of the boy.

"I'll cock-a-doodle you!" he yelled, and ran after Angelo.

Cock~a~doodle~doo!

This side, that side, round the stage
Pulcinella chased the little red rooster.
How the crowd cheered! They had
not seen such a lively performance
in years.

Finally, Zan Polo decided to stop
the show, with a flamboyant bow.

As soon as the crowds had gone, Zan Polo turned on Angelo.
"You have made my stage into a chicken yard with your
cock-a-doodle-doos!"

But even as he spoke, Zan Polo couldn't help smiling. The boy
looked just like his daughter's dreadful rooster Bardolino. He wanted
to laugh, but instead, he put on his sternest Pulcinella scowl and said,
"There is no place in my theater for a boy who will not listen or obey.
Now go!"

No sooner had Angelo gone than a gentleman wearing one red velvet glove approached Zan Polo.

"Buon giorno, Signor Polo. I am Nicolo Rossi, first secretary to the Rezzonico family," he said. "I am organizing a masked ball at the Palazzo Rezzonico, and it would be splendid if you would repeat your delightful performance for our guests tonight."

Zan Polo couldn't believe his ears. It had been many years since he had played before such a grand audience.

"And," said Signor Rossi, "be sure to bring the little red rooster with you. We would not miss him for the world."

Beneath his black mask Zan Polo reddened. Perhaps his grandson had the makings of a clown after all. Maybe he'd been too harsh with him . . . and now he thought of it, where was the boy?

As the evening shadows crept across the piazza, Zan Polo came across Angelo sitting against the column of San Marco's lion.

"I have been thinking, Angelo, that there might be a place in my theater for a boy like you."

Angelo's eyes widened with surprise.

"Do you mean I can be a clown?" he asked.

"That's what I've been thinking," said Zan Polo.

"And have my own special clown name?" asked Angelo.

"Zan Angelo has a good ring to it," said Zan Polo, smiling.

"May I do my cock-a-doodle-doo on the stage?" asked Angelo.

"Well, a *little* cock-a-doodle-doo would be nice," replied Zan Polo.

"In the middle of the stage?" asked Angelo.

"No, no, the side is a more suitable place for a cock-a-doodle-doo."

But Angelo was a chip off the old block. He said, "It's not what you play, it's how you play it that counts. And I want to do a *big* cock-a-doodle-doo right in the *middle* of the stage."

"We'll see, Zan Angelo," sighed the old clown, putting his arm around his grandson. "We'll see . . ."

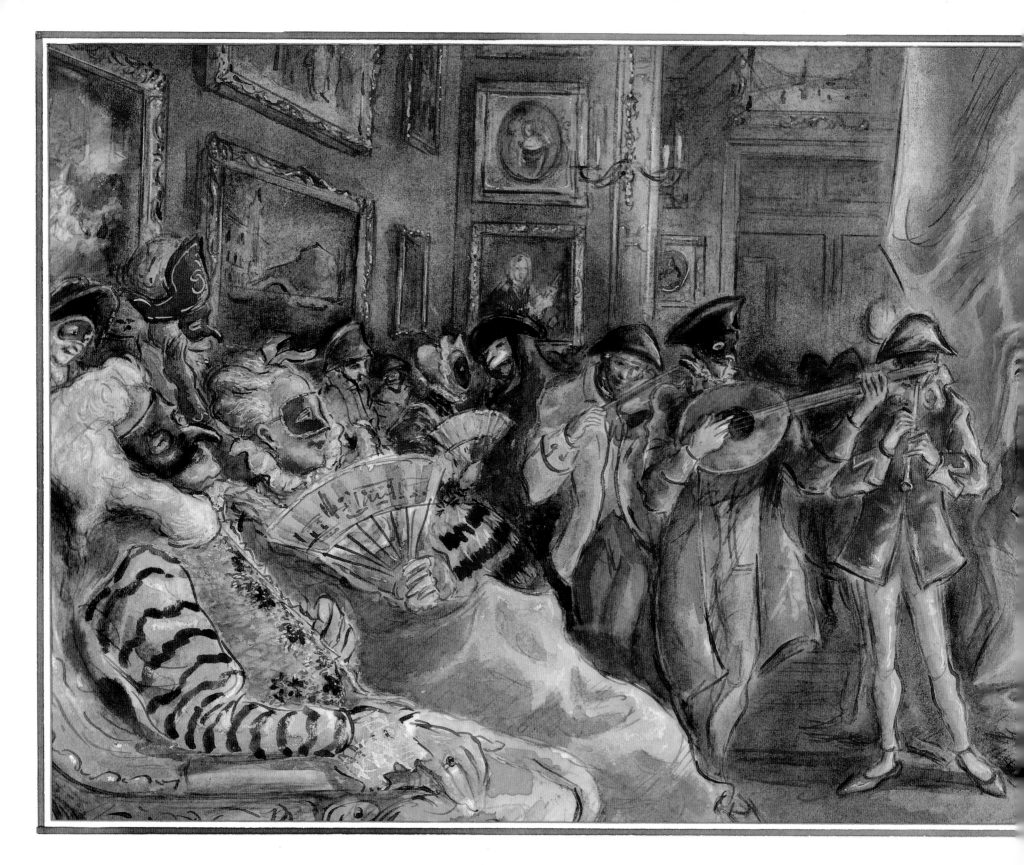

About Commedia dell'Arte

Toward the end of the fifteenth century, a new form of theater emerged in Italy: it was called *commedia dell'arte*. A comic form of street theater with its roots in Atellan farce and Greek mime, commedia dell'arte featured masked clowns called *zanni* playing characters such as Pulcinella, Arlecchino, and Pantalone.

In time, commedia dell'arte progressed from street to stage, and some actors used a shortened form of "zanni" in their stage names. Zan Polo was one of these. His spirited performances in the Piazza San Marco, recorded during the sixteenth century by the diarist Marin Sanudo, inspired this story; so too did the intriguing Pulcinella drawings of Giandomenico Tiepolo (1724–1804) and the festive paintings of Carnival life by Francesco Guardi (1712–93).

Although commedia dell'arte became less popular after the eighteenth century, its spirit lives on in the slapstick routines of stand-up comedians and clowns. Bravo!